Tales of
Tricksters

Also by Pleasant DeSpain

THE BOOKS OF NINE LIVES

VOLUME ONE

Tales of
Tricksters

Pleasant DeSpain

Illustrations by Don Bell

August House Publishers, Inc.
LITTLE ROCK

Published 2001 by August House Publishers, Inc.
P.O. Box 3223, Little Rock, Arkansas, 72203,
501-372-5450.

Printed in the United States of America

10 9 8 7 6 5 4 3 2 1 PB

LIBRARY OF CONGRESS CATALOGING-IN-PUBLICATION DATA
DeSpain, Pleasant.
  Tales of tricksters / Pleasant DeSpain ; illustrations by Don Bell.
    p. cm. — (The books of nine lives ; v. 1)
  Contents: Reynard and the fisherman (France) — Smuggler (Persia) —
Turkey and the fat mayor (United States) — Lindy and the forest giant
(Sweden) — Dancing wolves (Native American) — Alligator and the jackal
(India) — Rascal donkey (Switzerland) — Court jester (Poland) — That
tricky rabbit! (Native American)
  ISBN 0-87483-644-1 (alk. paper)
  1. Tricksters. 2. Tales. [1. Tricksters. 2. Folklore.] I. Bell, Don, 1935- ill. II. Title.
PZ8.1.D47 Taj 2001
398.2—dc21   2001022117

Executive editor: Liz Parkhurst
Project editor & designer: Joy Freeman
Copyeditor: Sue Agnelli
Cover and book illustration: Don Bell

AUGUST HOUSE   PUBLISHERS   LITTLE ROCK

For Eleanor J. Feazell and Edward E. Feazell,
my mother and stepfather.
You are loved and appreciated, always.

Acknowledgments

I'm fortunate to have genuine friends and colleagues without whose help, the first three editions of these tales would not have been possible. Profound thanks to: Leslie Gillian Abel, Ruthmarie Arguello-Sheehan, Merle and Anne Dowd, Edward Edelstein, Rufus Griscom, Robert Guy, Daniel Higgins, Roger Lanphear, Kirk Lyttle, Liz and Ted Parkhurst, Lynn Rubright, Mason Sizemore, Perrin Stifel, Paul Thompson, and T.R. Welch.

I owe allegiance and appreciation to the following for the newest incarnation:

  Liz and Ted Parkhurst, Publishers
  Don Bell, Illustrator
  Joy Freeman, Project Editor

The Books of Nine Lives Series

A good story lives each time it's read and told again. The stories in this series have had many lives over the centuries. My own retellings of the tales in this volume have had several lives in the past twenty plus years, and I'm pleased to witness their new look and feel. Originally published in "Pleasant Journeys," my weekly column in *The Seattle Times,* during 1977–78, they were collected into a two-volume set entitled *Pleasant Journeys, Tales to Tell from Around the World,* in 1979. The books were renamed *Twenty-Two Splendid Tales to Tell From Around the World,* a few years later, and have remained in print for twenty-one years and three editions.

Now, in 2001, the time has come for a new presentation of these timeless, ageless, universal, useful, and so very human tales.

The first three multicultural and thematically based volumes are just the beginning. Volumes four, five, and six will soon follow, and even more volumes are planned for the future, offering additional timeless tales.

I'm profoundly grateful to all the teachers, parents, storytellers and children who have found these tales worthy of sharing. One story always leads to the next. May these lead you to laughter, wisdom, and love. As evolving, planetary, and human beings, we are more alike than we are different, each with a story to tell.

—*Pleasant DeSpain*
Albany, New York

Contents

Introduction

Trickster is a marvelous, mischievous, and energetic character found in folktales from all around the world. Sometimes called Coyote or Turtle, sometimes named Rabbit, Fox, or Jackal, and sometimes a young girl or even an old man, Trickster takes on many disguises.

Trickster also does things that are both foolish and wise, often at the same time. Using tricks to help others, or teach lessons, or show that the world isn't always what it seems, Trickster plays a powerful role in society.

My favorite Tricksters are the smaller and seemingly weaker characters like Rabbit who uses wit and cleverness to survive predators like Wolf. I also like intelligent boys and girls who find ways to outsmart the bullies of the world, and create some fun along the way.

Trickster helps to bring the unfair world into balance through story. Here you'll find tales from France and Sweden, Poland and India. Two are Native American, and one is from ancient Persia, now called Iran.

Enjoy and share these nine tales, and let Trickster play. Long live Trickster!

Reynard and the Fisherman

France

Monsieur Reynard-the-Fox walked down to the river and decided to have fish for his supper. Since he lived by his tricks alone, Reynard walked until he came to an old fisherman putting his pole and worms into his cart. A long string of fat fish hung from his belt.

"That is my supper for tonight," thought Reynard.

The fisherman placed the fish in the back of his cart and climbed up to the seat. "Get up, Gigi," he said to the horse. "I want to be home before dark."

The fox trotted along the riverbank, careful to stay hidden in the trees. When he was far enough ahead of the fisherman's slow-moving cart, he lay on his back in the middle of the road with his feet pointing to the sky. He lay very still, his mouth open and his eyes closed.

Soon, the horse pulled the cart up to the fox and stopped.

"Gigi, why have you stopped? It is late and we must get home," said the fisherman.

But Gigi wouldn't budge, and the old man had to climb down from his seat to see what was wrong. His eyes opened wide when he saw Monsieur Reynard-the-Fox lying there.

"What's this? That tricky fox is dead? Wonderful! Now my chickens are safe. And his red fur will bring a high price at market. What a fortunate day!"

He picked up the fox, placed him in the back of the cart, next to the fish, and started on his way once again.

"When I sell the fox's fur," said the happy fisherman, "I'll use the money to buy a cow. The cow will have a calf and then I will be twice as rich. I'll sell them both and buy a small flock of sheep."

Meanwhile, Reynard licked his chops in the back of the cart and began to eat the fish.

"And then," continued the fisherman, "the sheep will have lambs. I can sell them and buy a new house. I'll turn the house into an inn and make so much money that I'll be able to buy the biggest store in town!"

Reynard swallowed another fat fish.

"So many people will shop at my store that I will soon be as rich as the king. Of course, I'll have to build a magnificent castle! I'll never have to fish again because I'll have one hundred servants and fifty cooks. I will eat wonderful meals from gold and silver plates!"

Reynard ate the last fish and stood up.

"Mr. Fisherman," he said, "since I have helped you become so rich, I trust that you will invite me to share your kingly spread."

The fisherman turned around. "But...but...but you're dead!"

"I'm dead? Then I must run home and tell my old mother. She will be very sad to hear it."

The fox leaped from the cart and started to run into the woods.

"Stop!" cried the fisherman. "I must have your fur. Without it, I will have nothing!"

Reynard kept running.

"Thief! Thief!" yelled the fisherman. "You are robbing me of my castle and my servants!"

The fox shouted back, "And I thought that I was only robbing you of your fish!"

With a sly grin and a full stomach, Monsieur Reynard-the-Fox ran home to his den.

The Smuggler

Persia

Once long ago, in Persia, there lived a trickster named Nasrudin. He was as clever as he was lucky, and he often took great risks.

One year he decided to smuggle goods between Persia and Greece. He tied two large baskets on his donkey's back and filled them with loose straw. Leading the donkey by a halter, he approached the Greek border.

"Here comes Nasrudin," said the captain to his guards. I'll bet he carries something illegal. Don't let him fool you."

The guards searched through the two large baskets of straw. They searched Nasrudin's donkey. Finally, they searched Nasrudin. They found nothing out of place.

"You may proceed," said the captain. "Don't try to bring anything back into Persia when you return."

"Thank you, Captain," Nasrudin answered. "Now that I know how good you are at your job, I won't try to deceive you."

Nasrudin crossed the border back into Greece late in the afternoon. A different group of soldiers were now standing guard. He walked up to the fresh captain, saying, "I have nothing to declare."

"Are you sure you're not bringing anything illegal into Persia?" asked the suspicious captain. "Perhaps you carry jewels hidden in your robe."

"Never," said Nasrudin, "You and your soldiers would find them and take them from

me. I'd have to spend time in jail. I wouldn't succeed at smuggling anything past your watchful eyes."

"Absolutely correct," replied the captain. "Guards, search him, and be thorough about it."

The guards searched Nasrudin and found nothing illegal.

And so it went, week after week. Nasrudin led his donkey across the border with two baskets filled with straw early in the morning, and returned home late in the afternoon. He and his donkey were searched crossing into Greece and he was searched again, coming home. Never once did the guards find anything wrong.

After fifty successful journeys across the border, Nasrudin decided to end his smuggling career. He became an advisor to the Persian ruler and, after many years of service, retired in luxury.

One day he was paid a visit by an old man. It was one of the former captains of the border guards, long retired.

"My mind has been troubled for many years, Nasrudin. It's a mystery that I want solved before I die. I know that you were a smuggler during the year that you crossed my border, but I still don't know what it was that you were smuggling. Please tell me."

Nasrudin smiled and answered with one word, "donkeys."

The Turkey and the Fat Mayor

United States

Once, an old man had a turkey who liked to strut up and down the road. The old man was so poor that he ate last night's potato skins for breakfast. One day the turkey found a gold nugget as large as your thumb lying in the middle of the road.

"Gobble, gobble, gobble. I'll take this to my hungry master!" said the turkey.

Just as he was heading home with the gold, the mayor happened to walk by. The mayor was fat. In fact, he was very fat. A skinny sheriff walked behind him, but you couldn't see the sheriff because the mayor was so fat.

When the fat mayor saw the turkey with the gold nugget, he said, "Turkey, I will take that gold home with me."

"No you won't," said the turkey. "It is for my old master, and he needs it more than you."

The fat mayor did not like to hear the word, "no." He ordered the skinny sheriff, "Get that gold for me!"

The sheriff chased the turkey down the road caught him by the neck, took the gold nugget away from him, and gave it to the mayor. The mayor took it to his home and put it in his large treasure chest.

The turkey was angry and followed the mayor to his house. Once there, he flew up to a window and called loudly, "Gobble, gobble, gobble, goo. Return my gold, or woe is you!"

The fat mayor became angry and called to the skinny sheriff, "Drown the turkey in the well!"

The sheriff caught the turkey and threw him into the well. But the turkey cried, "Oh, empty stomach of mine, drink up the water, and I'll feel fine!"

Sure enough, the turkey's stomach drank up all the water, and he flew back to the window and cried, "Gobble, gobble, gobble, goo. Return my gold, or woe is you!"

The fat mayor was even angrier than before and again called to the skinny sheriff, "Throw the turkey into the fireplace and burn him!"

The sheriff caught the turkey and threw him into the fireplace. But the turkey said, "Oh, stomach so big and so full, empty the water and save my soul!"

His stomach emptied and the fire went out.

He flew back to the window for a third time and cried, "Gobble, gobble, gobble, goo. Return my gold, or woe is you!"

The fat mayor was so angry that his face turned bright red. He called to the skinny sheriff, "Put the turkey on the hill of red ants and let the ants bite him to death!" The sheriff caught the turkey and placed him on the ant hill. The turkey cried, "Oh empty stomach of mine, eat all the red ants, and I'll feel fine!"

His stomach ate up the ants and he flew back to the window and cried, "Gobble, gobble, gobble, goo. Return my gold, or woe is you!"

The fat mayor was now so angry that steam came out of his ears! He didn't know what to do with the turkey. He called to the skinny sheriff and asked for his advice.

The sheriff said, "You could pull out all of his feathers...or you could cut off his head...or you could sit on him."

"That's just what I'll do!" said the fat mayor. "I'll sit on him! Bring him here!"

The sheriff caught the turkey and brought him to the fat mayor. The mayor placed him on a wide chair and sat down on top of him.

The turkey cried, "Oh, stomach so big and so full, empty the ants and save my soul!"

His stomach emptied and all the red ants began to bite the fat mayor. He jumped up from the chair and yelled, "Yeow, ouch, ohhh, ow! I have had enough punishment. Return the gold nugget to the turkey and send him home!"

The skinny sheriff opened the treasure chest.

The turkey looked inside and said, "Oh empty stomach of mine, eat all the treasure, and I'll feel fine!" His empty stomach ate up all the treasure, and now the turkey was fat!

He strutted home to his old master, and they lived happily and wealthily ever after.

Lindy and the Forest Giant

Sweden

The Forest Giant lived in a dark cave at the foot of Goat Mountain. He was a lazy and cruel giant who made the inhabitants of the valley below pay a heavy fine to live in peace.

Once each month the people had to drive a fat cow to the entrance of the giant's cave and leave it for him to eat. If a valley dweller wanted to fish in the nearby lake, he had to leave a big piece of cheese and one half of his catch for the Forest Giant.

If the people were late with their offerings

or tried to give him less than he demanded, he heaved huge boulders down on their houses and barns and stole their cattle during the night.

Everyone lived in great fear of the giant except for a clever girl named Lindy. Lindy never feared anyone or anything, and one day she decided to make the Forest Giant leave the valley. She picked up her fishing pole and line and walked to the lake. When she had caught six large trout, she walked up to the giant's cave and yelled inside, "Oh Forest Giant, full of fleas, here's three fish and some cheddar cheese!" And Lindy hurled four rocks into the darkness of the cave. The giant roared with anger and ran out of the cave. He was so large that he could have swallowed Lindy with one gulp. "How dare you mock me! Give me all of your fish or I will step on you!"

Lindy laughed and said, "Be calm, Uncle,

and speak softly, or I will have to break your leg."

"But I am big and strong," said the giant, "and you are only a little girl."

Now Lindy was angry and her eyes flashed. She pointed to a nearby tree and said, "Very well, Uncle, we will have a contest to determine who is stronger. Let's see who can make the largest hole in that tree, using only our heads!"

"I'll go first," said the giant, and he ran toward the tree with his head down. He hit the tree so hard that two squirrels were knocked to the ground, but there was no hole in the trunk.

"Ouch!" said the giant, as he rubbed his head. "I will try again!" This time he crashed into the tree so hard that the whole valley shook. The giant fell to the ground in a heap—he had knocked himself out!

Lindy quickly pulled some of the bark off

the tree, took an ax, and chopped a hole in the trunk large enough to put her head through. Then she placed the bark back over the hole.

Soon the giant woke up and said that his head was too sore to try again.

"Are you so weak, Uncle?" asked Lindy. "Let me have a turn and show you how it's done." She rammed into the bark where she had made the hole, and her head came clear out of the other side.

The giant, amazed by and afraid of Lindy's strength, said, "You may fish in the lake without paying me."

"Listen, Uncle," said Lindy. "Pay me for all the cattle, fish, and cheese that you have taken from the villagers, or I will squeeze you in half!"

"Come into my cave, and we will have some supper," replied the giant. "I will give you the money in the morning."

Lindy accepted the giant's invitation but realized that the giant would try to kill her during the night. She waited until he had eaten a huge plateful of fish and lay down to sleep. When he was snoring loudly, she crept out of the cave and found a small log. She carried the log back inside, covered it with a blanket and then hid behind a rock in the cave's darkest corner.

Soon after, the giant awoke. He picked up his ax and gave the log a heavy blow, thinking that it was Lindy under the blanket. Then he lay back down and started to snore once again.

Lindy tossed the log outside the cave. Then she lay down, pulled the blanket over her, and waited until morning.

When the giant opened his eyes and saw that she wasn't hurt, he became frightened and started to stutter. "DDDDid youuuu ssssleep wwwell?"

"Oh yes," said Lindy, "except for the little mosquito that bit me during the night. Now I'll take the money that you owe me."

The Forest Giant gave her a large bag of silver coins, and because he was afraid of Lindy's terrible strength, he moved away from Goat Mountain.

The villagers lived in peace forever after.

The Dancing Wolves

Native American (Cherokee)

Once, a rabbit walked through the woods on his way to visit the woodchuck. The woodchuck was his best friend and lived in a cozy hole under an old tree stump.

The rabbit was so pleased with the thought of his visit that he wasn't being careful to stay hidden in the brush and bushes. Suddenly, seven large and hungry wolves leaped out from behind seven trees and surrounded the rabbit.

"Rabbit," said one, "we are going to eat you for lunch!"

The rabbit was frightened, but he kept his wits and said, "But all of you can't eat me. I'm just a little fellow, only a mouthful. I agree that one of you should have me, but which one?"

The wolves began to argue among themselves, each claiming the rabbit.

"Stop!" said the rabbit. "I have thought of an idea that will solve the problem. Do you like to dance?"

"We love to dance!" said the wolves.

"Then let me teach you a new dance, and whoever dances best will win me for the prize!"

The wolves agreed and the rabbit described the dance.

"Since there are seven of you, the dance is in seven parts. First you line up, one behind the other. I'll stand by this tall tree and sing, and you dance away from me until I yell, turn! Then you turn around and dance back.

But stay in line!"

"We will! We will!" shouted the wolves.
The rabbit sang:

> *Dance, dance, dance,*
> *Each has a chance.*
> *Yum, yum, yum,*
> *Rabbit in my tum.*

The wolves danced away from him and kept their line straight. When the rabbit yelled, "Turn!" the wolves danced back and encircled him.

"Wonderful!" said the rabbit. "How beautifully you dance! For the second part, I sing from that other tall tree over there, and you dance as before, except that on every seventh step you turn one complete circle and chant 'Tibbar! Tibbar!'" (This is really "Rabbit! Rabbit!" spelled backwards.)

"This is fun!" cried the wolves.

The rabbit ran to the tall tree a little further away and sang his little song:

Dance, dance, dance,
Each has a chance.
Yum, yum, yum,
Rabbit in my tum.

And the wolves did their dancing and turning and chanting. When the, rabbit yelled "Turn!" they danced back to him.

"Magnificent!" said the rabbit as he ran even further away to the next tall tree. "That was much better than before! Now for the third part. Again you dance away from me, but this time you hop on every third step, clap your paws on every fifth step, and turn around on every seventh step."

And so it went, the rabbit moving from tree to tree with each part of the dance, and in doing so, getting closer and closer to the woodchuck's hole. The wolves had to concentrate harder and harder as each new dance became more complicated, and they began to forget about eating the rabbit.

When it was time for the seventh dance, the rabbit had moved very close to the woodchuck's hole.

The rabbit yelled, "This is the last dance, and it is the most fun! It is a racing dance and you must run away from me as fast as you can and turn a somersault on every tenth step. When I stop singing, and yell, 'Turn' you all race back. The first one to reach me gets me for lunch!"

The rabbit sang:

> *Rabbit for lunch!*
> *But I have a hunch,*
> *Whoever gets here first*
> *Will have nothing to munch!*

"Rabbit for lunch!" shouted the wolves, and away they ran, turning somersaults on every tenth step.

After the wolves were a good distance away, the rabbit yelled, "Turn!" and made a quick dash for the woodchuck's hole.

The wolves raced back, each one hungry for the rabbit. The rabbit, however, had vanished from sight.

Then, from under the ground, the wolves heard the last of Rabbit's songs:

Wolves can dance,
Wolves can prance,
And do funny things
When Rabbit sings!

The Alligator and the Jackal

India

Once a hungry jackal heard that an elephant had died on the other side of the wide river. He wanted to cross the river and feast on elephant meat, but he couldn't swim.

As he walked along the riverbank, he saw an old and rather large alligator sleeping in the sun. The jackal ran to a safe place and cried, "Wake up, mighty alligator! Time is short and your bride awaits!"

The alligator opened one eye and then the other. "My bride?"

"Oh yes," said the jackal. "There is a beautiful young alligator in the village on the other side of the river. She would make a splendid bride for you. Why not ask for her hand?"

"How would I do that, friend Jackal?"

"It is easy," said the jackal. "Simply carry me across the river on your broad back, and I'll make all the arrangements."

The alligator agreed and swam across the river with the jackal on his back. When they reached the opposite side, the jackal leaped onto the sand and said, "Return at sunset to carry me home, and I'll tell you of my success."

Then the jackal ran into the jungle and found the dead elephant. He ate all day long and was stuffed when the sun began to set. The alligator was waiting for him at the riverbank.

"When will she marry me?" he asked.

"I told her how strong and handsome you are," said the jackal, "and she was quite willing, and so was her mother and her brother. But her father wasn't home, so we will have to come again tomorrow to get his permission."

The next morning, the alligator gave the jackal another ride across the river and returned for him at sunset. The jackal, who had feasted all day on the elephant carcass, was waiting for him.

"Did her father agree?" asked the alligator anxiously.

"He wants to think it over," said the jackal. "He told me to return tomorrow for the answer. But his daughter is truly in love with you and is eager for the marriage."

And so it went. Each day the jackal invented a new delay and thus had an excuse to return to the other side of the river to dine on the elephant. When he had finally eaten

the last of the meat, he rode home on the alligator's back telling him tales of the maiden alligator's undying love for him.

When they arrived at the riverbank, the jackal leaped from his back and ran into the jungle. He then laughed long and loud, and cried, "Alligator, I have unfortunate news. Since you are really so stupid and ugly, the maiden doesn't want to marry you after all. But I want to thank you for the many rides across the river. You make an excellent ferryboat!"

The alligator was angry at being tricked and wanted revenge. After thinking about it for weeks, he came up with an idea.

He crawled into the deep jungle and found the jackal's den. He stretched out near the entrance, stiffened all of his joints, and lay there without moving. He was pretending to be dead.

Before long, the jackal returned and saw

the alligator. He stayed behind a tree and began to talk out loud to himself.

"Oh my, there is a dead alligator near my den. But wait, is he really dead? Dead alligators always curve their tails to the left, and this tail sticks out straight."

The alligator slowly curved his tail to the left.

The jackal laughed and ran into the jungle. From a safe distance he called, "Thank you, alligator, for showing me that you are still alive and still very, very stupid!"

The Rascal Donkey

Switzerland

Years and years ago, a retired professor
developed the habit of reading books
aloud, then falling asleep, while riding his
donkey. Sitting astride the donkey, heavy
book in hand, he kept his eyes on the page,
not the road.

The donkey had extra long ears and
intelligent black eyes. His snow white belly
contrasted nicely with his pearl gray hide.
He knew the way to town and rarely
wandered off into the green meadows.

The professor hoped that some of the

good words would rub off on the donkey.

"Listen closely, you old rascal. You could learn a thing or two from this..." and he would read aloud until he fell sound asleep, snoring all the way to town.

One of the professor's former students, a trickster at heart, decided to play a joke on his teacher. He asked a tall and rather strong stranger, passing through town, to help him out. The two lads hid in a thick grove of trees a half-mile from town, and waited until the sleeping professor rode by. They gently lifted the man from his beast of burden and set him on the stranger's back. The donkey was led away into the woods, while the youth carrying the professor continued on to town. The sleeping man soon awoke and was shocked to find that his donkey had turned into a man.

"I must be dreaming," he said. "My donkey may be a rascal, but surely he's not a demon.

What are you, friend or foe?"

"I'm a friend, professor. I used to be a thief. I was changed into a donkey for my punishment. You've read many good books to me and I've changed my ways. I've been forgiven and turned into a man, once again. Thank you, kind master."

"Then I must give you your freedom." He stepped down from the youth's back, saying, "Go on with your life and never steal again."

The lad ran into the woods and the professor turned around and walked back home.

The next day, the professor said, "I'll have to buy another donkey."

He walked to the open-air market and began searching for the perfect animal. There were many to choose from, large and small, young and old. Suddenly, he spied a donkey that looked familiar. It had extra long ears, intelligent black eyes, and a snow white belly in contrast to a pearl gray hide. It was his old donkey, now offered for sale by one of his former students.

"It's good to see you, Professor," said the youth. "Are you in the market for a donkey?"

"Yes, and this one is perfect. Is he expensive?"

"Not for you, Professor. You taught me well. I'll only charge you a dollar."

The professor happily paid, then whispered into the donkey's long ear, "You old rascal. Couldn't stop from stealing after all, could you? And look at you, changed back into a donkey again. I'll have to read twice as many books to you now."

He rode him home, reading from a good book along the way.

The trickster laughed long and hard.

The Court Jester

Poland

Once upon a time, an old jester entertained the royalty of a small kingdom. Joseph was his name, and when he was young, all of the court enjoyed his silly antics. The king and queen and the lords and ladies laughed for hours at his funny jokes and tricks. But now that he was old, his jokes fell flat and he received more yawns than applause.

Sadly, the king summoned Joseph. "My faithful clown," he said, "you have made us merry for many years, but the time has come for you to retire. I have had a small cottage built for you and your good wife, Anna. I will also give you a small bag of gold and wish you peace and comfort in your old age."

A tear rolled down Joseph's cheek, but he said, "As you wish, Your Majesty." He removed his colorful clown suit and funny cap with the long ears and little bells for the last time. Then, with Anna at his side and his head held high, he walked to his new home.

The small bag of gold was soon empty and Joseph and Anna grew hungry. They were too proud to beg, and because of their old age, no one would give them work. Soon they were desperate.

One day Joseph took his jester's rattle down from the shelf to dust it off, and an idea popped into his old head. "Anna," he said, "go to the queen and tell her that I died

in my sleep. Be sure to cry and carry on like a grieving wife."

The queen was shocked when she heard the sad news, for she had always liked the jester. "Poor Anna," she said, "please take this purse of gold. It will help to give our dear old joker a proper burial, and you can live on whatever is left."

Anna counted the gold as she walked home, and laughed out loud. One hundred gold pieces!

Joseph, too, was pleased, but added, "Now good wife, it is your turn to die. I will go to the king tomorrow and tell him the sad news."

Joseph put on a fine performance of sorrow and loss, and the King was touched.

"My dear old clown, how sorry I am for you. Take this small chest of gold and try to make a happy life for yourself."

Upon his return, Joseph found that the

king had given him three hundred pieces of gold. "Now we are rich, Anna! No longer will we starve."

Meanwhile the king and queen were having an argument. The queen said that the old joker had died, but the king explained that it was Anna, the jester's wife, who was dead. Finally the queen insisted on going to the jester's cottage to prove that she was right. The king agreed.

Joseph heard the approach of the royal coach and said, "Quickly Anna, let us lie down and pretend to be dead. You sprinkle some white flour on our faces, and I'll cover us with a sheet."

The king and queen walked into the cottage and saw the old couple lying side by side. The queen dabbed her eyes and the king blew his nose. Then the king said, "Joseph must have died from grief soon after Anna."

"No," said the queen. "Anna must have died from grief, just after Joseph."

"But Anna died first!" exclaimed the king.

"Joseph died first!" replied the queen.

"Excuse me," said Joseph as he sat up in the bed. "Let me explain. My wife died just before I did, but of course, I was already dead."

The king laughed long and loud and then said, "Explain this foolishness to me, jester."

Joseph told of how poverty had forced him to play his last trick, and the king and queen agreed that the old court jester and his wife should keep all of the gold that they had been given.

And so it was that Joseph and Anna lived in comfort until the end of their days.

That Tricky Rabbit!

Native American (Creek)

Wolf and Rabbit were friends until they met a pretty girl. The girl liked Wolf better than she liked Rabbit. Rabbit became jealous and told the girl that Wolf was actually his horse.

"He's not a horse. He's a wolf," she said.

"Will you believe me if I ride him to your place tomorrow?" asked Rabbit.

"Yes. Then I'll believe you."

The following day, Rabbit put a fake bandage on his foot, and knocked on Wolf's door. "Let's go visit that pretty girl."

"I'll race you there," said Wolf.

"Not today, my friend. I hurt my foot last night and can hardly walk. Will you carry me on your back?"

"All right," said Wolf. "You'll have to hold tight."

"It would be easier on both of us if you let me put my saddle and bridle on you."

"But I would look foolish carrying you like a horse."

"No one will see us. Besides, it will be fun!"

Wolf was in a good mood and agreed to the fun. Rabbit rode his new horse to the village of the People, and tied Wolf to a tree in front of the girl's lodge.

She came out and started laughing! "What an unusual horse you have, Rabbit. Come inside and share a meal."

Wolf stayed outside, tied to the tree. He was boiling mad.

Rabbit knew that Wolf would try to hurt

him when he finally untied him, and thought of a new plan while talking with the pretty girl. When the meal ended, Rabbit admired the girl's drum and asked if he could play it.

"Oh yes," she replied. "Play a warrior's song for me."

Rabbit began rapidly pounding on the drum-skin, faster and faster. It sounded like an army of horses heading their way.

"EEEEE!!!" yelled Wolf. "Untie me before the soldiers get me. Save me, Rabbit!"

Rabbit handed the drum to the girl and said, "Keep playing." He ran from the lodge and quickly untied Wolf. "Run," he cried, "Run for your life!"

Wolf sped into the nearby woods, not looking back even once, to see Rabbit and the girl laughing at their joke on him.

Wolf decided to destroy Rabbit, once and for all. He waited and watched for several days, until at last, he found Rabbit resting against a large rock. The rock lay near a cliff overlooking the People's village below.

Wolf began creeping toward Rabbit. Rabbit saw a movement from the corner of his eye and realized that he was in danger. Quickly placing his shoulder under the rock, he pretended to hold it back from rolling over the cliff.

"Say your prayers, Rabbit. You won't get away this time."

"That's just what I've been doing, friend Wolf. Thank goodness you've come along. I've been holding back this rock for hours. If it falls over the cliff, it will land on the lodge of the pretty girl. I can't hold it much longer. Squeeze in beside me and help me out."

Wolf didn't want anything to happen to the girl, and did as Rabbit asked. He pushed against the rock with all his strength. "How long do you think we can keep doing this?" he asked.

"Not much longer," panted the tired Rabbit. "You're strong enough to hold it back while I run down to the village and get ten strong warriors to help."

"All right, Rabbit, but hurry. This is a heavy rock!"

Rabbit eased away and ran down the hill. Wolf pushed against the rock with all his strength. He pushed and pushed, waiting for Rabbit and the ten warriors. He pushed until he was exhausted.

Rabbit didn't return with the warriors. Wolf, too tired to hold it back any longer, finally let go and leaped back. The rock stayed in its place. It didn't move an inch. It didn't roll toward the cliff. It rested solidly on the earth.

"Rabbit is so tricky!" yelled Wolf. "Just wait until I catch up with that tricky Rabbit!"

Notes

The stories in this collection are my retellings of tales from throughout the world. They have come to me from written and oral sources, and result from thirty years of my telling them aloud.

Six of these tales (indicated by asterisks) were previously included in my two-volume set entitled *Pleasant Journeys: Tales to Tell from Around the World* (Mercer Island, WA: The Writing Works, 1979), and later renamed *Twenty-Two Splendid Tales to Tell From Around the World,* (Little Rock: August House, 1990).

Motifs given are from *The Storyteller's Sourcebook: A Subject, Title and Motif Index to Folklore Collections for Children* by Margaret Read MacDonald (Detroit: Neal-Schuman/Gale, 1982).

Reynard and the Fisherman* — France

Motif K371.1. A model trickster tale, full of cleverness and fun, it's a delight to learn and tell. Role-playing, voices, and gestures add to the mix. Because adults enjoy it as much as children, I often share it in family programs.

Other versions are found in *Trickster Tales* by I.G. Edmonds (Philadelphia: Lippincott, 1966), pp. 99–102; and *Animal Folk Tales Around the World* by Kathleen Arnott (New York: Walck, 1970), pp. 79–82.

The Smuggler—Persia

Motif K409. I first heard this tale, framed as a riddle, while in graduate school. "He crosses the border each day, his donkey's baskets filled with straw. He returns home with baskets empty. What does he smuggle?" Years later I discovered it in a collection of Nasrudin tales. See *The Exploits of the Incomparable Mulla Nasrudin* by Idries Shah (New York: Dutton, 1972), p. 22.

The Turkey and the Fat Mayor*—United States

Motif Z52.4. Originating in the Middle East, this tale has traveled far and well. Children will naturally repeat "Gobble, gobble, gobble, goo. Return my gold, or woe is you!"

A Turkish version is found in *Favorite Stories Old and New* by Sidonie M. Gruenberg (New York: Doubleday, 1942, 1955), pp. 369–73.

For a Hungarian version, see *The Good Master* by Kate Seredy (New York: Viking, 1935).

Lindy and the Forest Giant*—Sweden

Motif K525.1. So often, it's a clever lad who is called upon to defeat the ogre. In this refreshing tale, Lindy proves more than equal to the task. Have fun portraying the foolish giant.

Another Swedish version: *The Boy Who Ate More Than the Giant and Other Swedish Folktales* by Ulf Löfgren, translated from the Swedish by Sheila LaFarge (New York: Collins and World, 1978), pp. 5–24.

A Norwegian version is found in *Norwegian Folk Tales* by Peter Christian and Jørgen Moe Asbørnsen (New York: Viking, 1960), pp. 81–87.

The Dancing Wolves* — Native American (Cherokee)

Motif K606.2.1. Escape by persuading the captors to dance and sing is a popular motif in Native American and Eskimo tales. Another Cherokee version has Groundhog escaping, rather than Rabbit.

See *John Rattling Gourd of Big Cove: A Collection of Cherokee Indian Legends* by Corydon Bell (New York: Macmillan, 1955), pp. 83–86; and *Cherokee Animal Tales* by George F. Scheer (New York: Holiday, 1968), pp. 31–32.

The Alligator and the Jackal* — India

Motif K1241.1. Tricking one who plays dead into giving himself away is a popular motif found in tales from around the world. An African version has Hare riding Leopard in search of a bride.

See *Grains of Pepper: Folktales from Liberia* by

Edythe Rance Haskett (New York: John Day, 1967), pp. 51–54.

A version from India is found in *Favorite Fairy Tales Told in India* by Virginia Haviland (Boston: Little, Brown, 1973), pp. 53–62. She discovered it in *Old Deccan Days; or, Hindoo Fairy Legends Current in Southern India* by Mary E. Frere (Philadelphia: Lippincott, 1868).

The Rascal Donkey—Switzerland

Motif K403.1. Jokes on absent-minded professors make good stories. I like that the former student charges his teacher so little for the return of his donkey. Even tricksters have a code of honor.

Another Swiss version is found in *The Three Sneezes and Other Swiss Tales* by Roger Duvoisin (New York: Knopf, 1941), pp. 16–19.

For a Spanish version, see *Three Golden Oranges and Other Spanish Folk Tales* by Ralph Steele Boggs and Mary Gould Davis (New York: McKay, 1936, 1964), pp. 39–46.

The Court Jester—Poland*

Motif J2511.1.2.1. I try to break my listeners' hearts with the king's genuine sadness as he retires his faithful jester. It makes the jester's final trick more poignant.

Two other versions: *Legends of the United Nations* by Francis Frost (New York: Whittlesey House, 1943), pp. 49–54. *The Crimson Fairy Book* by Andrew Lang (New York: Longmans, Green, 1903), pp. 158–67.

That Tricky Rabbit!—Native American (Creek)

Motif K500. Escaping by deception is prevalent in trickster tales. Using animals to tell a human courting story makes it even more fun.

I discovered this tale in *Teepee Tales of the American Indian* by Dee Brown (New York: Holt, Rinehart & Winston, 1979), pp. 106–9. He found it in *Myths of the Southeastern Indians* (U.S. Bureau of American Ethnology, Bulletin 88, pp. 63–66) Government Printing Office, Washington, 1929, as told by the Creeks to John R. Swanton about 1908.